Words
Every Teenager
Should
Remember

Blue Mountain Arts®

New and Best-Selling Titles

By Susan Polis Schutz:

*To My Daughter with Love
on the Important Things in Life*

To My Grandchild with Love

To My Son with Love

~

By Douglas Pagels:

*Always Remember How Special
You Are to Me*

The Next Chapter of Your Life

Required Reading for All Teenagers

Simple Thoughts

You Are One Amazing Lady

~

By Minx Boren:

Healing Is a Journey

~

By Debra DiPietro:

Short Morning Prayers

By Marci:

Angels Are Everywhere!

Friends Are Forever

10 Simple Things to Remember

To My Daughter

To My Granddaughter

To My Mother

To My Sister

To My Son

You Are My "Once in a Lifetime"

~

By Carol Wiseman:

Emerging from the Heartache of Loss

~

By Latesha Randall:

The To-Be List

~

By Dr. Preston C. VanLoon:

The Path to Forgiveness

Anthologies:

A Daybook of Positive Thinking

Dream Big, Stay Positive, and Believe in Yourself

God Is Always Watching Over You

Life Isn't Always Easy …but It's Going to Be Okay

The Love Between a Mother and Daughter Is Forever

Nothing Fills the Heart with Joy like a Grandson

The Power of Prayer

A Son Is Life's Greatest Gift

Strong Women Never Give Up

There Is Nothing Sweeter in Life Than a Granddaughter

There Is So Much to Love About You… Daughter

Think Positive Thoughts Every Day

Words Every Teenager Should Remember

Words Every Woman Should Remember

Focus on the journey, and never let a stumble in the road define who you are, where you are going, or how far you have come. It is important to slow down, enjoy life, and know that although the road you travel is yours alone, your present situation is not your final destination.

Sometimes the smallest step in the right direction ends up being the biggest leap of your life.

— Eileen Rosenfeld

Celebrate the Stars Shining in You

Be yourself; there's no one else like you. Celebrate your gifts. Appreciate each moment. Remember that for every hope there's a star, and for every star there's a wish that life will always be good to you. Open the treasures inside you, embrace every blessing, and welcome each new day.

See yourself as an amazing person. Your dreams are wonderful; live courageously and cast your doubts to the wind. There's more to life than our hearts realize, so do something that makes you smile every day.

Have faith that wishes come true all the time. Beautiful things happen when you believe. Search for rainbows. Accept yourself, recognize your uniqueness, and believe in your potential — no one does it quite like you.

Always listen to your heart and hear what your dreams are saying. Trust your instincts. Live in an extraordinary way: smile often, laugh a lot, and never lose sight of how special you are. Celebrate the stars shining in you and live your greatness.

— Linda E. Knight

Be Kind and Love Fearlessly

A little bit of kindness can go a long way
A little bit of laughter can brighten a day
A little bit of hope can plant a new seed
A little more love is all that we need

— Nina Heyen

Remember when you go into the world to keep your eyes and ears wide open. And be kind. Love one another. Take care of each other. Tell the truth. Always do your best.... Explore new paths and have fun. Know that you are loved like crazy. Give thanks for all your blessings. Above all else, love and you will do wonderful things in this world.

— Rebecca Puig

The majority of us lead quiet, unheralded lives as we pass through this world. There will most likely be no ticker-tape parades for us, no monuments created in our honor. But that does not lessen our possible impact upon the world, for there are scores of people waiting for someone just like us to come along; people who will appreciate our compassion, our encouragement, who will need our unique talents. Someone who will live a happier life merely because we took the time to share what we had to give.

Too often we underestimate the power of a touch, a smile, a kind word, a listening ear, an honest compliment, or the smallest act of caring, all of which have a potential to turn a life around.

— Leo F. Buscaglia

Be Patient with Others ...and Yourself

Be willing to listen;
    be open to the possibility
that things can be worked out,
because you can reach a compromise
    out of any conclusion.
Before you enter into
    a major debate,
take time to compose
    your thoughts and feelings.
Realize that anything
    and everything in life
has its own unique perspective,
and before you jump
    to any conclusions,
it's important to allow yourself
the time to completely understand.

— Deanna Beisser

Sometimes we don't know our power until the time comes to use it. It lies dormant within us and emerges just when we think we can't go on. And when it does, we find that we had much more power and strength than we ever thought possible.

So when you feel like giving up and throwing in the towel, know in your heart that your strength is on its way to the surface. One day you will look back at this moment and see just how strong you really were.

— Lamisha Serf-Walls

Remember who you are,
Who you want to become.
Everything will fall into place,
When the time comes.

— Dawn Jensen

It's Okay to Take Things Slow

When the world is moving on
And you're stuck in one place
Seeing your friends race ahead
While you struggle to keep pace
Close your eyes, shut off your ears
Breathe — learn to ignore them all
Feel the ground beneath your feet
Walk, as though you'll never fall.
Keep in mind the directions —
Only you know what they are
Have faith that your time will come
And soon, you'll have traveled far.

You will stumble, once or twice
There'll always be miles to go
Get up once more, try again
Keep marching on, as you grow.
If one day you reach your goal
Dream bigger, find a new aim
Help those climbing behind you
Don't forget from whence you came.

— Marya

One day at a time — this is enough. Do not look back and grieve over the past, for it is gone; and do not be troubled about the future, for it has not yet come. Live in the present, and make it so beautiful that it will be worth remembering.

— Ida Scott Taylor

We all require healing at one point or another. Take time to heal your wounds. Take time to heal your heart. It does no good to think about running the marathon when you still have a broken foot.

— Cleo Wade

Everyone is always on the move. People are moving forward, backward, and sometimes nowhere at all, as though they were on a treadmill. The mistake most people make is in thinking that the main goal of life is to stay busy. This is a trap. What is important is not whether you are busy but whether you are progressing; the question is one of activity versus accomplishment.

— John Mason

Embrace Each Day

Don't spend too much time looking in the rearview mirror. <u>Yesterday</u> is behind you. What's done is done, and it's important to take what you've learned from the experience and just move on.

<u>Today</u> is a brand-new opportunity, a blank canvas, an unwritten page in the diary. All that needs to happen right now is for you... to do the amazing things you're capable of.

<u>And tomorrow?</u> That's the place where promises come true. You'll need to be smart and stay strong to live the life you want to have. But don't ever forget: you are creative and capable and wise, and I know you have what it takes to make your days everything you want them to be. And remember this for sure...

You can't change a single thing about the past, but you can change absolutely everything about the future.

⌒ Douglas Pagels

Experience ALL You Can

Sing a new song; dance a new step; take a new path. Think a new thought; accept a new responsibility; memorize a new poem. Try a new recipe; plan a new adventure; entertain a new idea. Learn a new language; blaze a new trail; enjoy a new experience. Make a new friend; read a new book; see a new movie. Climb a new hill; scale a new mountain.... Find a new purpose; fill a new need; light a new lamp. Exercise a new strength; grasp a new truth; practice a new awareness.

Add a new dimension; encourage a new
growth; affirm a new beginning. Discover a
new answer; envision a new image; conceive
a new system. Dream a new dream; chart a
new course; build a new life. Open a new door;
explore a new possibility; capture a new vision.
Start a new chapter; seek a new challenge;
express a new confidence. Write a new plan;
turn a new page.... Watch a new program;
be a new person; radiate a new enthusiasm.

— William Arthur Ward

Live with Courage

Courage is the feeling that you can make it,
no matter how challenging the situation.
It is knowing that you can reach out
for help and you are not alone.
Courage is accepting each day,
knowing that you have the inner resources
to deal with the ordinary things
as well as the confusing things,
with the exciting things
as well as the painful things.
Courage is taking the time
to get involved with life, family,
and friends,
and giving your love and energy
in whatever ways you can.

Courage is being who you are,
being aware of your good qualities
and talents,
and not worrying about
what you do not have.
Courage is allowing yourself to live
as fully as you can,
to experience as much of life
as you are able to,
to grow and develop yourself
in whatever directions you need to.
Courage is having hope for the future
and trust in the natural flow of life.
It is being open to change.

— Donna Levine-Small

Seek Out People Who Lift You Up

There are some people in life who bring out the best in you. With them, you're able to say whatever's on your mind; you laugh and connect with them in a way that's so easy and unforced.

Around them, you can't help but feel happier, more full of energy, and ready to have some fun.

— E. D. Frances

Surround yourself with people who will support and encourage you and who make you feel good.

— Author Unknown

Cherish the ones who will be there
when you really need someone
and will come to you
when they need help...
who will listen to you
even when they don't understand
or agree with your feelings...
who will never try to change you
but appreciate you for who you are...
who don't expect too much
or give too little...
who will accept your attitudes,
ideas, and emotions,
even when their own are different...
who will be honest with you,
even when it might hurt,
and will forgive you for your mistakes...
who will support you
and who will bend over backward
to help you pick up the pieces
when your world falls apart.
They are life's most beautiful gifts.

— Luann Auciello

Be True to How You Feel

Good or bad, feelings need expression;
they must be recognized and given
freedom to reveal themselves.
It isn't wise to hide behind a smile
when your heart is breaking;
that is not being true to how
you feel inside.

Put away the myth that says
you must be strong enough
to face the whole world with a smile
and a brave attitude all the time.
You have your feelings that say otherwise,
so admit that they are there.
Use their healing power
to put the past behind you,
and accept them in your heart
as a part of you.
Use them to find peace within
and to be true to yourself.

— Barbara J. Hall

Never forget how to laugh
or be too proud to cry.
It is by doing both
that we live life to its fullest.

— Nancye Sims

Don't be afraid to feel what you're feeling.
Try to remember that you are not alone.
Remember that you are very loved, very
needed, and very special.

Life isn't always easy, but you are a
strong and beautiful person. You can get
through anything, and when you do, you
will be stronger and more amazing than
you already are.

— T. L. DiMonte

Don't Sell Yourself Short

Don't undermine your worth
by comparing yourself to others.
It is because we are different
that each of us is special.
Don't set your goals by what other people
    deem important.
Only you know what is best for you.
Don't take for granted the things closest
    to your heart.
Cling to them as you would your life,
for without them life is meaningless.
Don't let your life slip through your fingers
by living in the past or for the future.
By living your life one day at a time,
you live all the days of your life.
Don't give up when you still have something
    to give.
Nothing is really over until the moment you
    stop trying.

Don't be afraid to admit that you are less
   than perfect.
It is this fragile thread that binds us to
   one another.
Don't be afraid to encounter risks.
It is by taking chances that we learn how
   to be brave.
Don't shut love out of your life
by saying it's impossible to find.
The quickest way to receive love is to
   give love;
the fastest way to lose love is to hold it
   too tightly;
and the best way to keep love is to give
   it wings.
Don't dismiss your dreams.
To be without dreams is to be without hope;
to be without hope is to be without purpose.
Don't run through life so fast that you forget
not only where you have been,
but also where you are going.
Life is not a race but a journey to be savored
each step of the way.

— Nancye Sims

Love Yourself and the Rest Will Follow

It's hard to know how to get exactly what you want out of life. In the end, the trick is to love yourself.

Look in the mirror and admire the good qualities you have. Acknowledge the bad qualities and make a plan for how to improve them. Even if you never manage to change them, knowing you're trying gives you power over them and another reason to respect the person you are.

When you love yourself, it shows in the way you walk, talk, and treat other people. These positive manifestations you send out into the universe will start to bring good things back to you. Opportunities will present themselves. Things you have always wanted will be easier to find.

The secret to a happy life is simple: love yourself and the rest will follow.

— Joy Gorton

You Are Capable of More Than You Know

It's not silly to envision yourself
as being something greater than
what you are.
What is silly is believing that you
can't be greater in the first place.
Everyone who ever achieved
anything was first a person
who believed wholeheartedly
that they could
achieve something more.

— G. Boston

You are capable and worthy of being and doing anything. You just need the discipline and determination to see it through. It won't come instantly, and you may backslide from time to time, but don't let that deter you.

— Barbara Cage

When the challenges that lie ahead
seem too great to bear
and you don't know where you will get
the strength to carry on,
you will find a well of strength and courage
you never imagined you possessed.

With faith, love, and support,
you can walk through even the greatest trial.
Trust that you will have all you need
to get through any hard time, and remember...
you need only face one day at a time.

— Jason Blume

Set Goals for Yourself

Be an independent thinker
Make decisions
based on how you feel
and on what you know is right
regardless of what your peers
or other people think
Know yourself
Know what you can
and want to do in life
Set goals
and work hard to achieve them
Have fun every day in every way
Be creative —
it is an expression of your feelings
Be sensitive in viewing the world
Trust in your family
Believe in love —
it is the most complete
and important emotion possible
Believe in yourself
and know that you are loved

— Susan Polis Schutz

If you make your own goals
if you adhere to your own values
if you choose your own kind of fun
you are living a life made by you
If other people are telling you what to do
or if you are copying other people's ways
or if you are acting out a certain lifestyle
    to impress people
you are living for other people rather than
    for yourself

Do what you love
Control your own life
Have imaginative, realistic dreams
Work hard
Make mistakes but learn from them
Believe in yourself but know your limitations
Ignore all the naysayers
Plow through obstacles and failures
Turn your dreams into reality

— Susan Polis Schutz

There Are No Shortcuts to Any Place Worth Going...

If you focus on making one small change at a time, eventually those small changes will add up to one big transformation. Don't wait for the "perfect moment" to appear or when everything is "just right," or you may be standing still for the rest of your life.

It takes a leap of faith and some trust in the process to plant the seeds that will grow into a rewarding future. It takes courage to pursue your dreams and goals. Embrace the fear — it's only natural to be a little scared. It's a sign that we are ready to grow into the next chapter of life.

Now is the time for you to become the person you have always dreamed of becoming... now is the perfect time to make your dreams come true.

— Eileen Rosenfeld

Trust in Your Abilities

Trust your decisions and feelings
and do what is best for you.
The future will work itself out.
Don't let anyone else's negativity
influence your dreams, values,
   or hopes.
Focus on what you can change
and let go of what you can't.
You know your own worth
and what you're capable of.
Your goals may take a bit longer
and be harder to achieve
than you had hoped, but
concentrate on the positives
and combine faith with
generous portions of patience
and determination.
Step boldly and confidently
   into your future.

— Barbara Cage

Every day, remind yourself of all the things you are good at and all that you are capable of accomplishing in every area of your life. You are amazing in every way, and you should always remember that! Don't let other people discourage you from reaching for your dreams. What you do is up to you, because you are the only one who knows what you are capable of.

— Ashley Rice

Follow Your Own Path with Passion and Purpose

Don't ever forget that you are unique.
Be your best self
and not an imitation of someone else.
Find your strengths
and use them in a positive way.
Don't listen to those
who ridicule the choices you make.
Travel the road that you have chosen
and don't look back with regret.
You have to take chances
to make your dreams happen.
Remember that there is plenty of time
to travel another road —
    and still another —
in your journey through life.
Take the time to find the route
that is right for you.
You will learn something valuable
from every trip you take,
so don't be afraid to make mistakes.

— Jacqueline Schiff

Nothing great in the world has been accomplished without passion.

— Georg Wilhelm Friedrich Hegel

Live your life
with no regrets.
Reach for a dream
and make it your own.
Be brave enough
to invest a part of your heart
in something real that brings you
great pleasure.
Have a close circle of friends
and the love of family to share
all of life's special moments with.
Have a special sense of purpose
and an inner strength
that gives you the confidence
to face each new day
with boldness and courage.

— Cindy Chuksudoon

It Is Up to You

What you do with your life
    is your own choice.
How you decide to live your life
    and achieve your goals is up to you,
      and no one but you.
Mistakes will be made,
but you can learn from your mistakes.

Always remember to live your life
    in a way that's right for you.
Everything you do
should lead to your happiness,
and those who may at first disagree
    will hopefully, in time,
        be happy for you too.
Then you will come to see
    that the choices you make are right —
        if you make them for yourself.

— Jodi R. Ernst

Don't wait for what you want
	to come to you.
Go after it with all that you are,
knowing that life will meet you halfway.
Don't feel like you've lost
when plans and dreams fall short of
	your hopes.
Anytime you learn something new
about yourself or about life,
you have progressed.
Don't do anything that takes away
from your self-respect.
Feeling good about yourself
is essential to feeling good about life.
Don't let anyone hold your happiness
	in their hands;
hold it in yours, so it will always be
	within your reach.

— Nancye Sims

Dreams can come true if you take the time to think about what you want in life...
Get to know yourself
Find out who you are
Choose your goals carefully
Be honest with yourself
Find many interests and pursue them
Find out what is important to you

— Susan Polis Schutz

You make those big decisions.
You alone decide which path to take, what choice to make.

— Barbara J. Hall

Things Won't Always Go as Planned, and That's Okay

Life doesn't always happen the way you want it to. Detours suddenly appear; storms blow in unexpectedly. The road you're traveling — that seemed so safe and secure — changes direction without warning, and life becomes something that's not at all what you thought it would be. You find there's nothing to do but stop for a while, figure out your options, and think about new decisions you have to make.

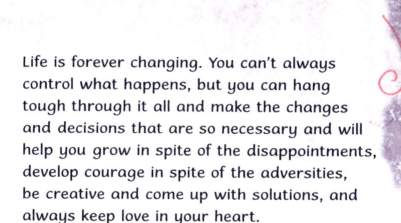

Life is forever changing. You can't always control what happens, but you can hang tough through it all and make the changes and decisions that are so necessary and will help you grow in spite of the disappointments, develop courage in spite of the adversities, be creative and come up with solutions, and always keep love in your heart.

No matter how hard things may seem... life will change again, and it's possible that one detour will lead you to a place that will bring you more happiness and let you reach more satisfying places in your heart and life than you've ever reached before.

— Donna Levine-Small

Fail Magnificently

Failure got me to the Olympics because it taught me to reinvent myself every day. It taught me to uproot all my bad habits and replace them with better ones. Failure got me to the Olympics because I learned how to capitalize on the opportunities when they came. It only takes one moment of success to realize that you are good enough.

You are going to "fail" the rest of your life. No one will know your lowest moments. No one cares, to be honest. They only want to be a part of your successes. They only want to see the good stuff. Everyone will tell you no, that you can't do it. Don't listen. They say that because they couldn't do it themselves. So ask yourself, how will you view failure? Will you view it as defeat or a chance to be better?

When you find yourself in the trenches of life, just know that every athlete you see on TV has been there too. In fact, they were probably sitting right next to you but you didn't notice. The only difference between you and them: they learned to love the trench life. They didn't avoid it; they took it as an opportunity to see what they are made of.

Success is gratifying, but it is your failures that you should value most. It is your failures that you should really grow fond of. Learn to thrive amongst failure and you have found how to succeed in life.

— Kate Hansen

Never Give Up

Life has a way of throwing us off course,
surprising us into making changes
we weren't planning on making.
Things may get difficult,
and you may struggle to do what's right.
But each new day brings new hope
and offers us a new chance to get it right.
Don't focus on what was.
Look forward to what can be,
and then do all you can to make it a reality.
Life is what you make of it,
and the challenges that come your way
are just opportunities to right what is wrong.
Don't get discouraged, and don't give up.
You have it all inside yourself,
and you can overcome anything
if you put your mind to it.

— Paula Michele Adams

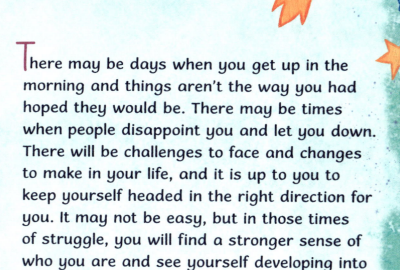

There may be days when you get up in the morning and things aren't the way you had hoped they would be. There may be times when people disappoint you and let you down. There will be challenges to face and changes to make in your life, and it is up to you to keep yourself headed in the right direction for you. It may not be easy, but in those times of struggle, you will find a stronger sense of who you are and see yourself developing into the person you want to be.

Life is a journey through time, filled with many choices; each of us will experience life in our own unique way. So when the days come that are filled with frustration and unexpected responsibilities, remember to believe in yourself and all you want your life to be, because the challenges and changes will only help you to find the dreams that are meant to come true for you.

— Deanna Beisser

Remember What Is Most Important...

It's not having everything go right;
it's facing whatever goes wrong.
It's not being without fear;
it's having the determination
    to go on in spite of it.
What is most important is not
    where you stand,
but the direction you're going in.
It's more than never having bad moments;
it's knowing you are always
    bigger than the moment.
It's believing you have already
    been given everything
you need to handle life.

It's the belief in your heart
   that there will always be
more good than bad in the world.

Remember to live just this one day
and not add tomorrow's troubles
   to today's load.
Remember that every day ends
and brings a new tomorrow
full of exciting new things.
Love what you do,
   do the best you can,
and always remember
   how much you are loved.

                — Vickie M. Worsham

Don't Take Life for Granted

Life can be so busy, and we sometimes take for granted the important little things that make us smile. Look at the sunset, share a cup of coffee with your best friend, or hear the wind rustle through the trees. Take some time to listen to life and feel the sun on your face. Stop to watch butterflies in your garden. Reflect on the past and all the memories, good and bad, that have made you who you are today. Your journey is far from over, as you will continue to grow, change, and flourish.

— Carol Schelling

Life is short. So do the things which make you happy. And be with people who make you happy. Look for the good in every day — even if some days you have to look harder.

— Karen Salmansohn

We spend so much time sweating the small stuff; worrying, complaining, gossiping, comparing, wishing, wanting, and waiting for something bigger and better instead of focusing on all the simple blessings that surround us every day. Life is so fragile, and all it takes is a single moment to change everything you take for granted. Focus on what's important and be grateful!

You are blessed, believe it!

Live your life and leave no regrets!

— Melanie M. Koulouris

Make Every Day Special

Make every day a day to celebrate life and be thankful. Take time to pull yourself away from all the noise and just look around you.

Take inventory. Appreciate those who have enhanced the quality of your life, and remember that they have been a gift to you. Also remember that you're a gift to them too.

Be grateful for the choices you've made, both good and bad. Accept your mistakes; you can't change them anyway. Appreciate yourself and your own uniqueness.

Go outside and look at the sky. Soak in the atmosphere. Enjoy the colors of the landscape. Feel the textures of every place you are that you're thankful for. Smile at the world. Don't allow any negative feelings to creep into your consciousness. Feel the power of your own acceptance. Put a positive spin on every thought you have.

Make every day special. Own it. Enjoy it. Bask in the glory of life. Appreciate the gift of your own life.

— Donna Fargo

Always Remember, You Matter...

Take a moment to think about
how many people have smiled
   because of you —
about all the lives you've changed
   for the better,
sometimes without even trying.

Take a moment to look back
at all the joy you've caused
and all the good you've done,
even when you thought you were
   at your worst.

Take a moment to remember
how much love you've sent out there
and how much you matter to people,
just because you're you.

Now think about yourself for a moment
and remember that you deserve
all the best in the world...
and so much more.

— Irina Vasilescu

You Are the Author of the Story of Your Life

It isn't always easy to make changes, but there's no better advice than this: just do your best. Make sure you stay strong enough to move ahead, because there are some wonderful rewards waiting for you.

It won't all make sense right away, but I promise you: over the course of time, answers will come, decisions will prove to be the right ones, and the path will be easier to see. Here are some things you can do that will help to see you through...

You can have hope. Because it works wonders for those who have it. You can be optimistic. Because people who expect things to turn out for the best often set the stage to receive a beautiful result.

You can put things in perspective. Because some things are important, and others are definitely not.

You can remember that beyond the clouds, the sun is still shining. You can meet each challenge and give it all you've got.

You can count your blessings. You can be inspired to climb your ladders and have some nice, long talks with your wishing stars. You can be strong and patient. You can be gentle and wise.

And you can believe in happy endings. Because you are the author of the story of your life.

— Douglas Pagels

Your Future Is Bright

Envision yourself succeeding. Imagine what you are going to accomplish, and then take the steps to actually achieve what you want to do. Keep your eyes on the prize at all times, and don't let any missteps discourage you in any way. Focus on the future and all you can do to make it unforgettable. You are irreplaceable and incredible, and there is no one else like you. Great things are coming your way — all you have to do is believe in yourself... and go for it!

— Ashley Rice

Be yourself, believe in yourself, try to love everything about yourself... and you'll be respected. ✎ Take care of your body and continue to challenge your mind... and you'll be admired. ✎ Don't listen to anyone who questions your dreams or your choices. ✎ Be your own leader... and others will follow you. ✎ Make the most of every moment, embrace every opportunity, and take lots of pictures... There's so much you'll want to remember. ✎ Take chances, trust your instincts, and celebrate every achievement — big or small. ✎ But most importantly, never give up on your dreams, because... you're going to love your future.

— Charley Knox

Acknowledgments

We gratefully acknowledge the permission granted by the following authors, publishers, and authors' representatives to reprint poems or excerpts in this publication:

Eileen Rosenfeld for "At times, we can get so caught up…" and "If you focus on…." Copyright © 2017 by Eileen Rosenfeld. All rights reserved.

Nina Heyen for "A little bit of kindness…" from ninaheyen.com, https://www.ninaheyen.com/news/random-acts-of-kindness-cards/. Copyright © 2022 by Nina Heyen. All rights reserved.

Sugaroo & Co. for "Remember when you go…" by Rebecca Puig, from sugarooandco.com, https://www.sugarooandco.com/remember-when-photobox/. Copyright © 2022 by Sugaroo Designs. All rights reserved.

SLACK Incorporated for "The majority of us lead…" from BORN FOR LOVE: REFLECTIONS ON LOVING by Leo F. Buscaglia. Copyright © 1992 by Leo F. Buscaglia. All rights reserved.

Deanna Beisser for "Be willing to listen…." Copyright © 2022 by Deanna Beisser. All rights reserved.

Dawn Jensen for "Remember who you are…" from "Remember," familyfriendpoems.com, February 2006, https://www.familyfriendpoems.com/poem/advice-to-live-by. Copyright © 2006 by Dawn Jensen. All rights reserved.

Marya (Marya123) for "When the world is moving on…" from "Slow," hellopoetry.com, August 2019, https://hellopoetry.com/poem/3270543/slow/. Copyright © 2019 by Marya. All rights reserved.

Cleo Wade (@cleowade) for "We all require healing…," Instagram image, November 17, 2019, https://www.instagram.com/p/B4_tdjtpNRQ/. Copyright © 2019 by Cleo Wade. All rights reserved.

Revell, a division of Baker Publishing Group, for "Everyone is always on the move…" from YOU CAN DO IT — EVEN IF OTHERS SAY YOU CAN'T by John Mason. Copyright © 2003 by John Mason. All rights reserved.

Donna Levine-Small for "Courage is the feeling…." Copyright © 2022 by Donna Levine-Small. All rights reserved.

Barbara J. Hall for "Good or bad, feelings need…." Copyright © 2022 by Barbara J. Hall. All rights reserved.

Gary Boston for "It's not silly to envision…" from "You Are Capable," *musings at random.* (blog), January 19, 2018, https://shadowofgevros.com/2018/01/19/quotes-you-are-capable/. Copyright © 2018 by Gary Boston. All rights reserved.

Jason Blume for "When the challenges that lie ahead…." Copyright © 2015 by Jason Blume. All rights reserved.

Kate Hansen for "Failure got me to the Olympics…" from "How failure got me to the Olympics," iamkatehansen.com, https://www.iamkatehansen.com/post/how-failure-got-me-to-the-olympics. Copyright © 2018 by Kate Hansen. All rights reserved.

Karen Salmansohn for "Life is short…" from "15 Life Is Short Quotes and Sayings to Motivate You to Live Fully," notsalmon.com, https://www.notsalmon.com/2019/01/02/life-is-short-quotes/. Copyright © 2019 by Karen Salmansohn. All rights reserved.

Melanie M. Koulouris for "We spend so much time…" from "Live with No Regrets," *Positive & Inspirational Quotes* (blog), May 16, 2013, http://positiveandinspirationalquotes.blogspot.com/2013/05/. Copyright © 2013 by Melanie M. Koulouris. All rights reserved.

PrimaDonna Entertainment Corp. for "Make every day…" by Donna Fargo. Copyright © 1997 by PrimaDonna Entertainment Corp. All rights reserved.

A careful effort has been made to trace the ownership of selections used in this anthology in order to obtain permission to reprint copyrighted material and give proper credit to the copyright owners. If any error or omission has occurred, it is completely inadvertent, and we would like to make corrections in future editions provided that written notification is made to the publisher:

BLUE MOUNTAIN ARTS, INC., P.O. Box 4549, Boulder, Colorado 80306.

Words
Every Teenager
Should
Remember

Inspiring Messages
to Guide Teens
on Their Journey
Through Life

A Blue Mountain Arts® Collection

Edited by Ellie Lindner
and Jessica O'Leary

Blue Mountain Press™
Boulder, Colorado

We wish to thank Susan Polis Schutz for permission to reprint the following poems that appear in this publication: "Be an independent thinker…," "Do what you love…," and "Dreams can come true if you take the time to…." Copyright © 1988, 2000, 2004 by Stephen Schutz and Susan Polis Schutz. And for "If you make your own goals…." Copyright © 1979 by Continental Publications. All rights reserved.

Library of Congress Control Number: 2022935184
ISBN: 978-1-68088-412-8

📖 and Blue Mountain Press are registered in U.S. Patent and Trademark Office.
Certain trademarks are used under license.

Acknowledgments appear on page 64.

Printed in China.
First Printing: 2022

♲ This book is printed on recycled paper.

This book is printed on paper that has been specially produced to be acid free (neutral pH) and contains no groundwood or unbleached pulp. It conforms with the requirements of the American National Standards Institute, Inc., so as to ensure that this book will last and be enjoyed by future generations.

Blue Mountain Arts, Inc.
P.O. Box 4549, Boulder, Colorado 80306

Contents

(Authors listed in order of first appearance)

Eileen Rosenfeld

Linda E. Knight

Nina Heyen

Rebecca Puig

Leo F. Buscaglia

Deanna Beisser

Lamisha Serf-Walls

Dawn Jensen

Marya

Ida Scott Taylor

Cleo Wade

John Mason

Douglas Pagels

William Arthur Ward

Donna Levine-Small

E. D. Frances

Luann Auciello

Barbara J. Hall

Nancye Sims

T. L. DiMonte

Joy Gorton

G. Boston

Barbara Cage

Jason Blume

Susan Polis Schutz

Ashley Rice

Jacqueline Schiff

Georg Wilhelm
    Friedrich Hegel

Cindy Chuksudoon

Jodi R. Ernst

Kate Hansen

Paula Michele Adams

Vickie M. Worsham

Carol Schelling

Karen Salmansohn

Melanie M. Koulouris

Donna Fargo

Irina Vasilescu

Charley Knox

You Are on an Amazing Journey

At times, we can get so caught up in reaching our destination that we forget to appreciate our journey. Life is filled with problems to solve, lessons to learn, and, most of all, experiences to enjoy.